Trouble on the carousel!

"The brass ring is missing!" Jo cried out. "It was right here, in front of the Partridge-in-a-Pear-Tree horse. Now it's gone. And the thief left this." She pointed a trembling finger at the horse.

Nancy leaned forward to take a closer look. There was a white piece of paper taped to the side of the horse.

It was a note! The note was written in red ink. Nancy stepped closer to read the words.

The handwriting was spooky-looking. The note said:

> Leave the horses alone. Or there will be more trouble.
>
> TG

The Nancy Drew Notebooks

Available from Simon & Schuster

THE
NANCY DREW
NOTEBOOKS®

#57

The Carousel Mystery

CAROLYN KEENE
ILLUSTRATED BY PAUL CASALE

Aladdin Paperbacks
New York   London   Toronto   Sydney

First Aladdin Paperbacks edition December 2003
Copyright © 2003 by Simon & Schuster, Inc.

ALADDIN PAPERBACKS
An imprint of Simon & Schuster
Children's Publishing Division
1230 Avenue of the Americas
New York, NY 10020

The text of this book was set in Excelsior.

Printed in the United States of America
10 9 8 7 6 5 4 3 2 1

Library of Congress Control Number 2003103453

ISBN 0-689-86342-X

1

A Holiday Surprise

I love parties!" eight-year-old Nancy Drew said from the backseat of her father's car.

"I *really* love parties!" her best friend George Fayne agreed. George was sitting next to Nancy.

"*I* love parties more than anything in the whole wide world!" George's cousin Bess Marvin piped up. Bess was Nancy's other best friend. She was sitting on the other side of George. "Except maybe presents. Hmm. I can't decide!"

Nancy, George, and Bess all lived in River Heights and were in the same third-grade class at Carl Sandburg Elementary School.

The three girls were on their way to a holiday party at Nick and Patricia Gangi's house. The Gangis were friends of Nancy's dad, Carson Drew. Mr. Drew was also their family lawyer.

"The best thing about the holidays is that you get parties *and* presents," Nancy said from the front seat.

"And no school for two whole weeks," George added.

Outside the car, snow was falling softly. Nancy pressed her face against the window and stared at the scenery. She liked seeing all the houses decked with holiday decorations and holiday lights.

Mr. Drew turned onto a road lined with snow-covered trees. Just ahead was an enormous gray mansion. Beyond it was a big white meadow that ended in a stretch of woods.

"Is that their house?" George exclaimed.

"It's like a princess's castle!" Bess nodded.

"Dad, you said this party had a super-secret surprise theme," Nancy said eagerly. "What is it? Can you tell us?"

"You'll find out soon enough," Mr. Drew promised with a chuckle.

Nancy couldn't wait. *What could the super-secret surprise theme be?* she wondered.

Mr. Drew parked the car behind a long row of cars in the driveway. As the four of them walked up to the house, the snow made crunching sounds under their boots.

On the front door there was a big wreath made of twigs, dried cranberries, origami paper birds, and tiny silver bells. Under the wreath was a handmade sign that said COME IN! in purple and green crayon.

Nancy and her friends followed Mr. Drew inside. The front hall and living room were filled with grown-ups and kids. Servers in black uniforms walked around with trays of food and drinks.

"Welcome, welcome!"

A tall man with light brown hair rushed to greet them. He was wearing a green velvet jacket with a sprig of mistletoe on the lapel.

Mr. Drew shook the man's hand. "Girls, this is Mr. Nick Gangi," he said.

Nancy, George, and Bess all shook hands

with Mr. Gangi. "Is this whole house yours?" George asked, her brown eyes wide.

Mr. Gangi laughed. "Yes, this whole house is ours. It first belonged to my great-great-grandfather, Thomas Gangi. In fact, he's sort of the reason for this party." He winked at Mr. Drew.

Nancy glanced at her father, and then at Mr. Gangi. *Mr. Gangi must be talking about the super-secret surprise theme,* she thought.

"I know he lived a really long time ago, but was today your great-great-grandfather's birthday?" Nancy guessed

Mr. Gangi smiled. "No, but that's a good guess. Why don't all of you come with me into the living room. I was just about to make my announcement. Plus, I want you to meet the rest of the family."

Mr. Gangi led Mr. Drew, Nancy, George, and Bess into the crowded room. Everyone was standing around, talking and eating.

In the corner of the living room, Nancy saw a giant Christmas tree. It was covered with twinkling white lights, strings of popcorn, carved wooden dolls, and many other beautiful decorations.

While Nancy gazed at the tree, a pretty woman with long, wavy, dark brown hair walked over to them. Two blond girls stood next to her, one on either side. Nancy guessed the girls were about her age. Just behind them was a red-haired teenage boy.

The two girls looked almost exactly alike. The only difference was that the first girl wore her hair in a ponytail. The second one wore her hair down, with lots of purple barrettes. *They must be twins,* Nancy thought.

"Hi, Patty," Mr. Drew said. He kissed the woman on the cheek. "Girls, this is Mrs. Gangi," he said.

"These are my daughters, Johanna and Mia," Mrs. Gangi said. "And this is their cousin Brad Gangi," she said, pointing to the red-haired teenager.

The girl with the ponytail pouted. "*Jo*, not *Johanna*," she insisted.

"This is *Jo*," Mrs. Gangi corrected herself with a smile. "Jo and Mia's little brother, Sam, is around here somewhere. You can't miss him. He's wearing a Turtleman T-shirt."

Bess plucked a chocolate cupcake off a

server's tray. "Turtleman? I *love* Turtleman. He's awesome."

"Turtleman is lame. Just like this party is lame," Nancy heard Brad mumble to Mia.

"Brad! Shut up!" Mia snapped.

"But I know how to make the party way cooler," Brad whispered to both Jo and Mia. "You want to help me?" He had a mischievous look in his eyes.

"Shhhhh," Jo and Mia whispered together.

Nancy wondered what *that* was all about. But she didn't have time to think about it; just then, Mr. Gangi clinked a spoon against a glass.

"Can I have everyone's attention?" he called out in a loud voice. "Attention, everyone! I have an announcement to make."

Nancy turned to George and Bess. "Yay, this is it!" she whispered.

Everyone in the room fell silent. Mr. Gangi put the spoon and glass down. Then he stuffed his hands into his jacket pockets and began to give a speech.

"A hundred years ago, my great-great-grandfather, Thomas Gangi, lived in this house with his wife and three children," Mr.

6

Gangi said. "He was a craftsman who made carousel horses. He was famous all over the world for his horses."

"Carousel horses, that's so cool!" George whispered. Nancy nodded.

"Thomas Gangi made a special carousel for his children," Mr. Gangi went on. "It used to be on the grounds of this house."

Nancy wondered where the carousel was. She didn't remember seeing it out front.

"The carousel was taken down a long time ago," Mr. Gangi continued. "No one knew what became of the horses . . . until now."

Mr. Gangi held his hands out to his daughters, Jo and Mia. The two girls went to stand on either side of him.

"One rainy day last spring, our two girls were playing hide-and-seek in the basement," Mr. Gangi explained. "While they were playing, they found a secret room! Patty and I didn't know this house even *had* a secret room. But inside the secret room, Jo and Mia found the twelve carousel horses!"

Nancy gasped. *What an awesome discovery,* she thought.

Nancy liked to solve mysteries. In fact, she had solved lots of mysteries with Bess and George. But they had never come across missing carousel horses in a secret room!

Mr. Gangi smiled down at his daughters. "I immediately hired a carousel expert. He restored the horses to their original condition. Then our family decided to donate the horses to the city of River Heights. The carousel will be unveiled at a grand opening in the park on Wednesday—and it's all thanks to my two little girls!"

Everyone in the room burst into applause. Nancy clapped and cheered.

Then she noticed something. Mia looked kind of nervous. She was fiddling with her barrettes and staring down at the ground. Nancy guessed Mia didn't like all the attention she and Jo were getting.

Then Nancy noticed a little boy with brown hair peeking out from behind the velvet couch. He was wearing a Turtleman T-shirt and had a big frown on his face.

That must be Sam Gangi, Nancy thought. *But why does he look so unhappy too?*

"The twelve horses are on display in our

library," Mr. Gangi announced. "I wanted all of you to get a chance to see them first before we hand them over to the city. Then, on Wednesday, a group of lucky children will get the first ride. They'll get to participate in a special contest, too. Whoever gets the brass ring wins a prize!"

"What's a brass ring?" Bess asked Nancy. Nancy shrugged.

"Some carousels have a brass ring, some don't," Mr. Drew explained. "It's a big ring that hangs from the side of the carousel. You grab for it while the carousel is going around and around. Whoever grabs it first usually wins a prize."

"It sounds fun!" Nancy said.

"Please, please, follow us!" Mr. Gangi said loudly. "It's time to see the horses—and the brass ring, too. The brass ring has a hand-carved design on it. It's the only one like it in the whole world."

Mr. Gangi, Jo, and Mia led the way into the library. The crowd shuffled after them, talking in excited voices.

"I can't wait to see the horses!" Bess said, jumping up and down.

"I can't wait to—," Nancy began.

But she was interrupted by a couple of loud screams from the library. It sounded like Jo and Mia!

2

A Ghostly Note

Nancy, George, and Bess rushed into the library through the double doors. Nancy's thoughts were racing. *Why did Jo and Mia scream? Were they hurt? What happened?*

A crowd had already gathered in the library. Nancy squeezed through a bunch of grown-ups to the front so she could see what was happening. George and Bess did the same.

Mr. and Mrs. Gangi, Jo, and Mia were at the front of the crowd. No one seemed hurt. But Jo and Mia looked like they were about to start crying.

"Oh, my gosh!" Bess gasped. "Nancy, look!"

Nancy glanced around.

Lined up along two walls of the library were a dozen old-fashioned carousel horses.

The horses were painted different colors—white, beige, pale pink, sky blue, yellow, brown—with lots of shiny gold trim. Each one had its own design. The first one had a picture of a bird in a pear tree on it. The second one had a picture of two birds nestled close together. The third one had three brown hens. . . .

"It's 'The Twelve Days of Christmas,'" Nancy said.

"Who screamed? What happened?" one of the guests demanded.

"The brass ring is missing!" Jo cried out. "It was right here, in front of the Partridge-in-a-Pear-Tree horse. Now it's gone. And the thief left this." She pointed a trembling finger at the horse.

Nancy leaned forward to take a closer look. There was a white piece of paper taped to the side of the horse.

It was a note! The note was written in red ink. Nancy stepped closer to read the words.

The handwriting was spooky-looking. The note said:

Leave the horses alone. Or there will be more trouble.

TG

Bess peeked over Nancy's shoulder. "Who's TG?" she demanded.

Mia read the note too—and gasped. "TG? That must be our great-great-great-grandpa, Thomas Gangi!"

"Isn't he . . . um, dead?" George asked her.

Jo gasped. "It must be his ghost, then! His ghost left this note!" She turned around and rushed into her mother's arms. "Mommy, I'm scared!"

Mia also ran into her mother's arms. "Me too, Mommy!"

Sam stood behind his father. He picked at a big chocolate stain on his Turtleman T-shirt. He looked pretty scared too.

"This was *not* the work of a ghost," Mr. Gangi murmured. "Ghosts don't exist."

"There are no such things as ghosts,"

15

Nancy agreed. "Someone may be *pretending* to be a ghost, though."

"I'm sure there's a reasonable explanation for all this," Mrs. Gangi said. "Maybe this is someone's idea of a joke."

Everyone in the room was whispering about the missing brass ring and the note. The party had gone from super-fun to super-mysterious in less than a minute!

Mr. Gangi asked two of the servers to escort the guests out of the room. "We'll get this straightened out," he announced to the crowd with a big, cheerful smile.

The guests shuffled out the door. Mr. Drew, Nancy, George, Bess, and the whole Gangi family stayed in the library.

Mr. Gangi turned back to Mr. Drew. His smile faded into a frown.

"This is not good," he said in a low voice to Mr. Drew. "My great-great-grandfather made that brass ring specially for these carousel horses. It was one of a kind."

"And now there won't be anything for the children to grab on Wednesday for the contest!" Mrs. Gangi added. "Oh, Nick! What could have happened to the brass ring? And who left that note?"

"Nancy can find out for you!" Bess exclaimed.

Mr. and Mrs. Gangi looked at Bess in surprise. "What do you mean?"

"Nancy's an awesome detective," George piped up. "She's solved lots of mysteries."

"I'd be happy to help," Nancy offered.

Mr. Drew put his arm around Nancy's shoulders. "With you on the case, honey, I'm sure we'll solve this mystery in no time," he said with a smile.

"If you can help us find that brass ring by next Wednesday, we'd sure appreciate it," Mr. Gangi said.

"Nancy'll catch the thief!" Bess said.

"You mean the ghost," Jo said. Mia nodded.

"There are no such things as ghosts," Nancy repeated.

Just then, Nancy noticed someone sitting on a velvet couch in the corner. It was Brenda Carlton. She was dressed in a red satin dress with a big bow at the collar. She was scribbling like mad in a small notebook.

Brenda was in Nancy, Bess, and George's third-grade class. Her father was the publisher of the River Heights newspaper.

Nancy had always tried to be friendly to Brenda. But Brenda could be snooty and mean sometimes. She thought she could do just about anything better than anyone—including Nancy!

The Gangis were talking to Mr. Drew about the brass ring. Nancy excused herself and walked over to Brenda.

Brenda glanced up. As soon as she saw Nancy, she closed her notebook shut.

"I'm busy," Brenda announced before Nancy could say a word.

"Um, hi to you, too, Brenda," Nancy said cheerfully. "I didn't know you were at this party."

"My father knows the Gangis. My father knows everybody," Brenda replied in a huffy voice.

Nancy was curious. Why did Brenda stay in the library when everyone else went back to the living room? Was she snooping on the conversation between the Gangis, Carson, Nancy, Bess, and George? And what was Brenda writing in her notebook?

Nancy sat down on the velvet couch next to Brenda. She leaned over and pointed to the notebook. "What are you writing?" she asked. "It's not homework, is it? We're on vacation, remember? We don't have school till January!" she joked.

"It's none of your beeswax," Brenda snapped. "All I can say is that what I'm writing is important. *Really* important."

Without saying good-bye, Brenda jumped to her feet and pranced out the door, toward the living room.

Nancy frowned. *Does Brenda know something about the missing brass ring?* she wondered.

And then she thought of something else. *Where was Brad Gangi?*

"He's not in our room," Jo Gangi said. "He's not in Sam's room either."

Jo, Mia, Nancy, Bess, and George had spent the last twenty minutes looking for Brad. First they had combed the first floor. But they had not found Brad with the rest of the guests.

Now they were upstairs looking through the bedrooms. But Brad didn't seem to be in any of them, either.

"Maybe he went home or something," George suggested.

"No way. Mom and Dad haven't served the big flaming Christmas cake yet. Brad would never miss that," Jo said.

"Flaming . . . cake?" Bess repeated. "You mean it's on fire?"

"Why are we looking for Brad, anyway?" George asked Nancy.

"I heard him whispering to you guys," Nancy said to Jo and Mia. "He said he had some plan to make the party 'way cooler.' What if he meant stealing the brass ring?"

Jo and Mia glanced at each other. Jo began twirling her ponytail. "I *guess*," she said slowly.

"Brad *is* kind of a jerk," Mia agreed.

"Do you guys know if he's ever stolen stuff before?" Nancy asked the sisters.

Mia shrugged. "I think he might have stolen one of Sam's baseball cards once," she said after a minute.

Jo gasped. "Hmm. Maybe he *did* steal the brass ring."

Mia nodded. "Yeah, maybe."

"What a jerk!" Jo said in an angry voice.

"He's just a suspect, for now. We have to get some proof first," Nancy pointed out.

The five girls continued down the hall. They came upon the Gangis' master bedroom. Inside, the king-size bed was heaped with coats and bags.

Mia pointed to a yellow and black parka that was on the floor. "That's Brad's," she said. "He must still be here."

Nancy noticed a black backpack next to the parka. It was covered with faded motorcycle stickers.

It also had the initials BG on the front pouch, in red.

"Is this Brad's backpack?" Nancy asked.

"Yup!" Mia said, nodding.

"Maybe the brass ring is in there," Bess whispered to Nancy. She glanced over her shoulder at the door. "Maybe you should open it!"

Nancy didn't know what to do. She didn't

want to poke through Brad's backpack. On the other hand, what if Brad was the thief? What if the brass ring was in there?

Nancy picked up the backpack and turned it around in her hands. She tried to feel for the brass ring through the outside of the pack.

She could feel some books. She could also feel something else—something round.

She started to unzip the zipper.

"What do you think you're doing?" a voice demanded.

3

Big News

Nancy's head shot up at the sound of the voice. Brad was standing in the doorway!

Sam was right behind him. He was holding a cup of fruit punch. Some of it had spilled down the front of his Turtleman T-shirt.

"What are you doing with my backpack?" Brad demanded.

He stormed into the room and grabbed the backpack out of Nancy's hands. He looked really mad.

Nancy tried to think up a good excuse. "Um, we were just—," she began.

"We were just looking for the brass ring

that you stole," Mia cut in. "Where is it? Give it up, Brad!"

"Yeah!" Jo said.

"The . . . the what?" Brad frowned. "You mean that thing that goes with those horses? Why would I steal that?"

"You said before that you had some plan to make the party 'way cooler,'" Nancy reminded him. "'Way cooler'—like stealing the brass ring and making everyone think a ghost took it?"

Brad laughed. "What? Oh yeah, right. As if I would come up with something that lame."

"Then what *did* you mean?" George asked.

Brad laughed again. "I put something in the punch."

Sam stopped drinking his punch and stared at his cup. "What did you put in it?" he asked Brad in a scared-sounding voice.

"Don't worry, Samster the Hamster; it was *after* you got your punch," Brad reassured him. "Just minutes ago, I dumped some of my extra-special ice cubes in the silver punch bowl."

"What extra-special ice cubes?" Bess asked.

"Ice cubes with spiders in them," Brad explained.

Just then, there was a high-pitched scream from downstairs. Then a voice yelled, "There's a spider in my punch!"

"Pass the popcorn!" Bess said to Nancy.

"Pass the cider," George said to Bess. "We'd better make sure there are no spiders in it first!" she joked.

"Ha-ha," Nancy said.

Nancy sat up in her sleeping bag and passed Bess the popcorn bowl. It was Saturday night, and Bess and George were having a sleepover at Nancy's house. Nancy loved sleepovers!

Nancy was wearing her new pajamas that had tiny pink hearts on them. Bess was wearing red pajamas with white lace trim. George was wearing her blue and green plaid pajamas and fuzzy blue slippers. The three girls had spread their sleeping bags across Nancy's bedroom floor.

Nancy licked popcorn butter off her fingers. Then she picked up her blue notebook, which was lying on the floor.

Her father had given her the blue notebook for solving mysteries. For each mystery,
Nancy kept track of suspects and clues on
a different page in the notebook.

She turned to a clean white page. She
picked up her purple pen and wrote:

The Mystery of the Missing Brass Ring

"You should write down all our suspects
first!" Bess said eagerly.

"*All* our suspects?" Nancy repeated. "I
think we only have one, so far."

"You mean Brad?" George asked her.

Nancy nodded. "Yup."

Nancy made a column with the heading
"Suspects." Then, underneath, she wrote:

Brad Gangi: He likes to play pranks. He
wouldn't let us see what was inside his
backpack.

"I really think he's the thief," Bess said,
munching on a handful of popcorn.

"We can't blame Brad without any proof,"
Nancy reminded her.

Nancy made another column with the heading "Clues." Underneath that, she wrote:

The thief left a note. It was in red ink. It said, "Leave the horses alone. Or there will be more trouble. TG."

George took off one of her fuzzy blue slippers and threw it across the room. It landed in Nancy's basket of stuffed animals. "Two points!" she hooted. "Anyway, what do you think that means, 'Leave the horses alone'?" she asked Nancy and Bess.

"Maybe the ghost doesn't want the horses to go to the park," Bess suggested.

"It's not a ghost, Bess. It's someone *pretending* to be a ghost," Nancy told her.

Bess shrugged. "Whatever."

Nancy nibbled on the end of her pen. "Maybe the thief just wanted the brass ring because it's valuable. Maybe the note is just a smoke screen."

"A smoke . . . what?" George asked her.

"A smoke screen. It's detective language. It means when a criminal leaves a clue that's supposed to confuse you," Nancy explained.

"Well, it worked, because I'm totally confused!" Bess said, frowning. "More popcorn, please!"

The next morning, Nancy woke to the sound of Hannah's voice coming up the stairs:

"Rise and shine, girls! Who wants pancakes?"

Hannah Gruen was the Drews' housekeeper. But she was more like one of the family. She had been helping take care of Nancy since Nancy's mother died five years ago.

Nancy, George, and Bess all jumped out of their sleeping bags and raced downstairs. The yummy smell of pancakes and butter and maple syrup wafted up from the dining room.

Mr. Drew and Hannah were already at the table. "Good morning, Pudding Pie," Mr. Drew said to Nancy. "Pudding Pie" was his special nickname for her. "Good morning, George and Bess. Everyone sleep well?"

"Yes, Mr. Drew!" George and Bess said at the same time.

"There's blueberry pancakes and a few strawberry pancakes, too," Hannah said.

George and Bess started to eat. Nancy took a sip of her orange juice. She noticed that the Sunday newspaper was spread all over the table. She glanced at it quickly— then she saw something *really* strange.

Nancy grabbed the paper. There was a small column on the front page of the B section. It was called "Kids' Korner."

Underneath those words was a black-and-white picture of Brenda Carlton. Next to her picture was the headline:

BRASS RING STOLEN AT GANGI HOME
CITY CAROUSEL DOOMED!

4

Nancy Has Competition

Nancy couldn't believe it. Brenda had written a big, fat article about the missing brass ring for her father's newspaper!

"What are you looking at, Nancy?" Bess asked through a mouthful of pancakes.

Nancy pointed to the article. "Look! It's an article by Brenda!"

Bess and George leaned over Nancy's shoulder.

"The beginning is all about how Jo and Mia found the horses and the brass ring," Nancy explained. "I'll read the good part."

Nancy began to read:

"Everyone was enjoying the Gangis' party. There was lots of yummy food, like cookies and cupcakes. But then tragedy struck! There was a scream from the library. Someone had stolen the brass ring and left a spooky note on one of the horses. The note said 'Leave the horses alone. Or there will be more trouble. TG.' The brass ring was one of a kind. It had a mistletoe design on it.

"TG are Thomas Gangi's initials. Did he come back as a ghost to steal his own brass ring? Is he trying to tell us something about the horses? Are there clues to this mystery behind the old blue door of the secret room? Stay tuned!

"This article was written by ace reporter and detective Brenda Carlton."

"A detective!" Bess burst out. "Brenda is not a detective!"

"And when did she become a reporter for her dad's paper?" George added. She speared a piece of pancake with her fork and stuffed it into her mouth.

32

Nancy read the article over again. "So that's what Brenda was doing in the library," she said finally. "I caught her writing something in her notebook. It must have been this story!"

Nancy frowned. "I'm confused. Brenda wrote something about an old blue door going to the secret room. How does she know about that? Mr. Gangi didn't say anything about it. And how did Brenda know that there was a mistletoe design on the brass ring?"

George stopped chewing. "You're right, Nancy!" she exclaimed.

"We'd better go find Brenda and talk to her," Nancy said.

Later that morning, Nancy, Bess, and George walked into the Double Dip. The Double Dip was their favorite ice-cream parlor in town.

But this time, ice cream wasn't their main mission. They were looking for Brenda. Nancy had called Brenda's house to talk to her about her article. Brenda's mother, Mrs. Carlton, had told Nancy that Brenda and her best friend, Alison Wegman, were hanging out at the Double Dip.

"There she is!" Bess whispered, pointing.

Nancy and her friends walked over to them. Brenda and Alison were eating ice-cream sundaes.

"Hey, Brenda. Hey, Alison," Nancy said.

Then Nancy did a double take. Alison was eating a pink bubble-gum sundae. Brenda was working on a blue bubble-gum sundae . . . and a hot fudge sundae . . . and a peanut butter crunch sundae . . . and a pineapple partytime sundae . . . and a strawberry surprise sundae . . . and a ragin' rainbow sundae, too. Six sundaes in all!

"S-s-six s-s-sundaes?" Bess stammered. Her blue eyes were huge.

Brenda flipped her dark hair over her shoulder. "Yes, six sundaes! I'm writing a food review for my dad. He wanted me to do an article about the best ice-cream sundae at the Double Dip."

"You are *so* lucky," Nancy said.

Brenda smiled smugly. "It's talent, not

luck. My dad knows I'm the best kid reporter in River Heights."

"And the best detective," Alison added helpfully.

George stepped forward. Her fists were in knots. Nancy could tell she was about to argue with Brenda about her "best detective" comment.

Nancy quickly stepped in front of George. "You really are an awesome reporter, Brenda!" she said.

Brenda looked pleased. "Thanks!"

"We read your article about the brass ring in today's paper," Nancy said. "You wrote about stuff no one else knew about. Like the old blue door in the basement. And the mistletoe design on the brass ring. How did you find out about those things?"

Brenda sat up a little taller. "Well, it wasn't easy. But a good reporter can find out anything! See, what I did first was talk to—"

And then Brenda stopped. She glared at Nancy. "Hey, I know what you're doing," she said suspiciously. "You're using me to help you solve this mystery, aren't you?

Well, forget about it, Nancy Drew! I'm going to solve this mystery first. And then I'm going to write all about it for the 'Kids' Korner' column!"

5

A Spooky Song

I have a new suspect for our mystery," Bess said. "Brenda Carlton!"

"Yeah! Add her to the suspect list!" George agreed.

It was after lunch on Sunday. Nancy, Bess, and George were walking to the park with Hannah. Hannah had Nancy's puppy, Chocolate Chip, on a leash. The little Lab puppy kept stopping and sniffing everything along the way, like trees and bushes and snowmen and snow women.

Nancy stuffed her hands into the pockets of her parka. "Why do you think Brenda should be a suspect?" she said with a frown. "I mean, she's trying to solve the case—just like us!"

"That's why," Bess said. "Maybe Brenda stole the brass ring and left the note—"

"—so she could write a story about it for her dad's newspaper. And so she could pretend to solve the mystery and look like a big hotshot," George finished.

"You girls certainly have a case on your hands." Hannah sighed. "Chip, where do you think you're going?" she cried out. The puppy was trying to race after a squirrel.

Nancy thought about Bess's and George's words. At the Double Dip, Brenda had bragged that she would solve the mystery before Nancy did. And Brenda would, if she had stolen the ring!

On the other hand, stealing was a really bad thing to do. Would Brenda go that far to be the number one kid detective in town?

The girls, Hannah, and Chip arrived at the park.

"Let's check out where the carousel will be!" Nancy suggested.

The carousel structure was nestled in the trees in the middle of the park. It had see-through glass walls and a peaked roof made of pretty gray stone. There was an old-fashioned sign at the entrance that said WELCOME TO THE RIVER HEIGHTS CAROUSEL. ONE RIDE: 50 CENTS.

Nancy pressed her nose against the glass and peeked in. There were hammers and nails and cans of paint scattered all over the floor. It looked sad and empty without the carousel horses and brass ring.

Nancy was determined. She *had* to find the brass ring in time for the grand opening on Wednesday!

"I think this one's my favorite," George said. She pointed at the carousel horse with seven swans on it. "Seven swans a-swimming!"

"I like this one the best," Jo said. "Five golden rings!"

It was Monday afternoon. Hannah had dropped Nancy, Bess, and George off at the Gangis' house so they could look for more clues. The three girls had searched all over the first and second floors with a fine-tooth comb. So far, they had turned up nothing.

Now they were in the library, checking

out the horses. Nancy realized once again how beautiful they were. Each one was painted a different pretty color with shiny gold trim. Each one had its own design on it from the song "The Twelve Days of Christmas." And each one also had a long, bushy tail, just like a real horse.

Then Nancy got an idea. She lay down on the rug and rolled onto her back. She scooted under the belly of one of the horses.

"Nancy, what are you doing?" Bess asked.

"Do you want a flashlight or something?" Mia offered.

"Yes, please!" Nancy replied.

Mia disappeared, then came back a moment later with a flashlight. Nancy clicked it on. She swept the beam of light to the right, then to the left.

Nancy was about to turn the flashlight off when something caught her eye. On the horse's underside were two red, hand-painted letters: TG.

"Hmm," Nancy said out loud.

"Did you find something, Nancy?" George asked her.

"Maybe," Nancy replied.

While the four girls watched, Nancy scooted under each horse and shined the flashlight around. All the horses had the initials TG on them, just like the first one.

A few minutes later, Nancy got up and brushed her hands against her jeans. "All these horses have the initials TG on them," she announced to the others.

"Those are the initials of our great-great-great-grandpa!" Jo said.

Nancy nodded. "And the handwriting is the same as it was on the note. Which means that whoever left the note knew what Thomas Gangi's handwriting looked like."

"Or the person who left the note *was* Thomas Gangi," Bess said in a nervous voice.

Nancy shook her head firmly. "No way."

"I still think Brad is the thief," Mia said. "I don't know why you don't just have him arrested or whatever."

"We don't have any proof against him yet," Nancy pointed out.

The girls took a quick break to have Christmas cookies and hot chocolate. Then Mia excused herself because she had to get ready for her violin lesson. "You guys keep

looking around without me," she said.

"But we've looked all over the house," Bess said, munching on a cookie. "And we didn't find anything except for a bunch of initials."

"You haven't looked *all* over the house," Mia called out over her shoulder as she left the kitchen.

"That's true! We haven't looked in the basement yet," Jo pointed out. "Don't you want to see the secret room where we found the horses and the brass ring?"

Nancy nodded. "That's a great idea!"

"But what if the ghost lives down there?" Bess said nervously.

"Bess! There are no ghosts!" Nancy reminded her.

"I agree with Bess. I think ghosts are totally real," Jo said.

"Well, ghost or no ghost, we should still check out the basement," Nancy declared.

The girls finished their snacks. Then they headed down to the basement. Nancy took the flashlight with her.

The basement was dark and musty-smelling. There were cardboard boxes, dusty old furniture, and broken toys everywhere.

"This way," Jo said, leading the girls through a narrow doorway.

They found themselves in a small, dimly lit room. Nancy felt cobwebs brushing against her bare arms. She shivered.

Jo pointed to a small wooden door on the far wall. The blue paint on it was chipped and faded. "That's the door Mia and I found last spring," she said in a low voice. "No one knew it was there because a bunch of cardboard boxes were piled in front of it. It leads to the secret room."

The four girls walked carefully to the door. Jo reached out to open it.

Just then, Nancy heard a noise. "What's that?" she whispered.

It sounded like music coming through the door. The music was scratchy and spooky-sounding.

"It's . . . it's a song," George said nervously.

Nancy recognized the song. "It's 'The Twelve Days of Christmas'!" she exclaimed.

6

A Musical Clue

It's the ghost of Thomas Gangi!" Bess cried out. "He's playing 'The Twelve Days of Christmas' because he wants us to leave his carousel horses alone!"

"Shhh," Nancy whispered. She put her finger to her lips. The music stopped.

Nancy reached out to open the door to the secret room. It wouldn't budge.

"Jo, help me!" Nancy said.

"It gets stuck sometimes," Jo explained. She jiggled the doorknob. After a minute the door swung open. The hinges creaked.

Nancy rushed through the door into the secret room. She swung the flashlight around. The room looked empty. "Is there a light in here?" she asked Jo.

"No," Jo replied. "Dad's been meaning to put one in, but he hasn't gotten around to it yet. Can we leave now?" Her voice trembled.

Nancy kept shining the flashlight around. There was an old cabinet with chipped paint, a couple of broken rocking chairs, and a pile of cardboard boxes. That was all.

But then Nancy shined the flashlight on the far corner of the floor. She saw a few pairs of muddy footprints.

Nancy rushed over to the footprints and knelt down. Next to one of the prints were the initials TG, written in mud.

Jo leaned over Nancy's shoulder and gasped. "The ghost was here!" she cried out. She looked really scared.

"Ghosts don't wear shoes," George said.

"*This* ghost does," Bess said in a shaky voice.

Nancy frowned. Someone was definitely trying to make them think there was a ghost. First there was the note in the library. Then there was the spooky music, the footprints, and the muddy initials.

The sound of something falling startled the girls. "What was that?" Bess demanded.

The sound had come from outside the secret room. Nancy jumped to her feet and ran out the door.

Sam Gangi was in the outer room. Near him, there was a cardboard box lying upside down on the floor, next to a pile of other cardboard boxes. *He must have knocked it down by accident*, Nancy thought.

"What are you doing here?" Nancy asked.

Sam stared at Nancy with wide green eyes. "Wh-what? N-nothing. I was looking for my, um, old Turtleman cards."

"They're not down here," Jo snapped.

"Mom put them somewhere, and I can't find them," Sam insisted.

"Liar, liar, pants on fire," Jo taunted him.

Sam glared at his sister.

"Hey, Sam," Nancy said in a friendly voice. "Do you have a portable CD player? Were you just playing music down here?"

"No!" Sam burst out. Then he turned around and ran up the stairs.

"*Why* do I have to have the weirdest

brother in the whole world?" Jo said with a loud sigh.

Nancy frowned. *Sam is acting like he's afraid,* she thought. *Did he have something to do with the music or the muddy footprints or the initials? Did he steal the brass ring?*

"He's acting kind of strange," Nancy agreed. "But let's go! I have an idea!"

Brad opened the front door as soon as Jo rang the doorbell. He frowned at his cousin. Then he turned to frown at Nancy, Bess, and George, who were standing behind Jo.

"What do you want?" Brad asked impatiently. "I'm right in the middle of a major Video Warriors championship."

"We, uh . . ." Jo quickly glanced at Nancy.

"Jo wanted to know what she and Mia should get your parents for Christmas," Nancy fibbed.

Brad looked confused. "Huh?"

"This'll only take a minute," Nancy said. She stomped her snowy boots on the doormat and stepped inside the house. Jo, George, and Bess did the same.

Nancy was glad she'd thought of the idea

to pay Brad a visit. He and his parents lived only a few doors away from the Gangis.

Brad was still a suspect in their mystery. And Nancy wanted to look through his house for clues—particularly clues having to do with the spooky song and the muddy footprints. Nancy had drawn a rough sketch in her notebook one of the muddy prints.

Inside the living room, Jo began chattering to Brad about gift ideas for his mother and father. "Mia and I were thinking about a cookbook. What do you think? Let's see which cookbooks your parents already have." She grabbed Brad's arm and yanked him down the hallway.

"Quick, start looking around. We don't have much time," Nancy whispered.

"What are we looking for, exactly?" Bess whispered back.

"Muddy shoes. 'The Twelve Days of Christmas.' Anything that seems suspicious," Nancy explained.

George nodded. "Okey-dokey."

The three girls split up. George took the living room and hall closet. Bess took the dining room. Nancy went upstairs to check out the bedrooms. If Brad caught her, she would just tell him that she was looking for the bathroom.

Nancy tiptoed down the carpeted hallway. She came upon a half-open door. It had a handwritten DO NOT DISTURB sign on it.

Nancy peeked in. It was someone's bedroom. There were motorcycle posters on the walls. There were clothes scattered all over the floor. The desk was covered with soda cans, potato chip crumbs, and piles of books and magazines.

This must be Brad's room, Nancy thought.

Nancy noticed a pair of black-and-white sneakers on the floor. She pulled her notebook out of her pocket and turned to the page with the footprint drawing out on it. Then she picked up one of the sneakers and compared it to the drawing.

Nancy's raced. The sneaker and the footprint drawing were the same size!

Just then she heard George in the hallway. "Nancy? Are you in there?" George called out.

Nancy poked her head outside. "I'm here. What's up?"

George was standing there holding something shiny in her hand. It was a CD. "Nancy, we've solved the mystery!" she whispered excitedly. "Take a look!"

George held the CD out to Nancy. The name of the CD was *The Best of Christmas*.

The first song on the CD was "The Twelve Days of Christmas"!

7

To Catch a Thief

Nancy glanced at the CD again. Then she showed George the sneaker and the footprint drawing.

"Brad's got to be our thief!" George said.

Nancy nodded. "He looks pretty guilty. Let's go talk to him."

Nancy and George raced downstairs. Bess, Jo, and Brad were all in the dining room.

"Oh, *there* you are," Bess said in a loud, nervous voice. "I was just telling these guys that you were in the bathroom."

Nancy handed the CD to Brad. "Does this look familiar?" she asked him.

Brad stared at the CD. "Uh, no. It's

probably my mom and dad's. The only CDs I own are Megabreath and Galactica."

"We think you stole the brass ring and left that spooky note," George blurted out. "Today, you tried to scare us by hiding in the secret room and playing this CD. You even left your muddy footprints there!"

"I did . . . *what*?" Brad seemed totally confused. "Secret room? Muddy footprints? Have you guys been reading too many mystery comic books or what?"

"The footprints match your shoe size," Nancy told him.

Brad shrugged. "Big deal. There's probably, like, thousands of people with the same shoe size as mine. Besides, why would I steal that stupid brass ring?"

"Because you like to play mean pranks," Joe cried out. "Like how you put spiders in the punch."

"*That* was cool. Stealing some old piece of metal is *not* cool," Brad replied.

Nancy frowned at Brad. Was he lying about the brass ring? Or was he telling the truth? It was impossible to tell.

***

"So how is your case coming along, Pudding Pie?" Mr. Drew asked Nancy.

They were baking holiday cookies together. The kitchen was filled with the smells of sugar and cinnamon. Through the window, Nancy could see snow falling softly against the dark blue evening sky.

Nancy squirted some white icing along the outline of her gingerbread girl. "Okay, Daddy," she said. "We have a few suspects."

"Who?" Mr. Drew asked.

"Well, our number one suspect is Brad Gangi, who is Jo and Mia and Sam's cousin," Nancy replied. She told her father all about the music and muddy footprints in the secret room. "Brad's shoe size matches the footprints," she finished. "Plus, we found a CD with that song at his house."

"That's good detective work, Pudding Pie," Mr. Drew said with a smile. "Still, don't forget: Lots of people have Christmas CDs."

"I know." Nancy nodded. "And lots of people have the same shoe size as Brad's," she added. "Brenda's a suspect too. She might have stolen the brass ring so she

could pretend to solve the mystery and look like a hotshot. Sam's kind of a suspect too."

"Little Sam Gangi?" Mr. Drew looked surprised. "He's only six years old. Why do you think he would steal the brass ring?"

Nancy picked out a piece of red candy to make the gingerbread girl's nose. "I'm not sure. He was acting strange at the Gangis' house today. Maybe he's jealous because his sisters have been getting lots and lots of attention about the horses."

Mr. Drew's hands were covered with powdered sugar. He wiped them on a dish towel and said, "Here's another idea: What if someone stole the brass ring because it's valuable?"

Nancy nodded slowly. "Hmm. I thought about that too. I think you're right, Daddy!"

Mr. Drew's comment gave Nancy an idea. "May I use your computer to do research on the Internet, Daddy?" she asked her father. "Maybe I can find out more stuff about brass rings."

Mr. Drew smiled. "Great idea, Pudding Pie. Let's go to my study."

The two of them washed their hands,

then headed down the hall to Mr. Drew's study. Nancy loved her father's study. It had a big wooden desk with his computer and other work things on it. Nancy often liked to sit next to her father and draw while he typed on the computer.

Mr. Drew and Nancy sat down at the desk. He had a special work chair, and she had a smaller one just like it.

Mr. Drew spent a few minutes booting up his computer and typing in some commands. Then he scooted over so Nancy could surf the Web.

Nancy found a page called Kidsearch and typed in the word "carousel." She knew that the Kidsearch program would find a bunch of Web pages that were related to carousels.

A few minutes later a picture of a carousel flashed up on the screen. The carousel had at least thirty horses.

"It's so big!" Nancy said, her blue eyes wide. "I wish I could go for a ride on it."

"Sure, Pudding Pie. But let's hope we'll have our very own carousel right here in River Heights," Mr. Drew reminded her.

Nancy scrolled down the screen. "Here's

some information about brass rings. Oh, and here's something about Thomas Gangi," she said excitedly.

Nancy quickly glanced at the page. "It says here that there are only three of his brass rings in the world," she told her father. "That means that all three of them must be super-valuable! Oh, and it says that Thomas Gangi sometimes put a secret compartment in his carousel horses."

"Really?" Mr. Drew said.

Nancy continued to surf the Web. She learned that one of Thomas Gangi's brass rings was in Paris, France. The other one was in South Africa.

While she was surfing, Nancy thought . . . and thought . . . and thought.

After a while, something occurred to her—something brilliant!

"Daddy!" she exclaimed. "I think I know exactly how to catch our brass ring thief!"

8

Brass Ring Bust

Okay, so what's the big emergency?" Bess asked Nancy. "I had to race through my Strawberry Crunch cereal to get here."

"We're really curious!" George added.

It was Tuesday morning. Nancy, Bess, and George were sitting at the Drews' dining room table.

Last night, Nancy had come up with a plan to catch the thief. She had told her father right away. He had agreed that it was a great idea.

Now she had to run her plan by her two best friends. After all, she needed their help to pull it off!

Nancy began talking excitedly. "My dad and I did some research on the Internet last night. We found out that there are only two other Thomas Gangi brass rings in the world. One of them is in a museum in Paris, and the other one is owned by a millionaire in South Africa."

"Wow," Bess said.

"So here's the plan," Nancy went on. "What if I get all our suspects together in one room? I'll make believe that everything is fine now because my dad found one of the other Thomas Gangi brass rings in an antique store close to here. I'll tell them that we're going to use it as a substitute at Wednesday's ceremony."

"I don't get it," George said. "You said the other Thomas Gangi brass rings were in Paris and South Africa. How is your dad going to get one of them here by tomorrow?"

"He's not," Nancy explained. "We're just going to *pretend* that Dad found the brass ring in an antique store."

Bess's blue eyes lit up. "I get it! You're hoping that the thief will try to steal the pretend brass ring by tomorrow."

Nancy nodded. "Yup! I'll act like I'm putting it somewhere in the Gangis' house and I'll let everyone know where it is. And maybe, just maybe, someone will try to steal it."

George gave Nancy a high five. "You're the smartest detective I know, Nancy!"

It was Tuesday afternoon. Nancy glanced around the Gangis' living room. Everyone was there: George, Bess, Brenda, Brad, Jo, Mia, and Sam.

Sunlight slanted through the large bay windows and fell across the room. In the corner, the small white lights on the Christmas tree twinkled and danced. A fire blazed brightly in the fireplace.

Nancy took a deep breath. She wondered if her plan would work. Would the thief give himself or herself away by trying to steal the pretend brass ring?

"Okay, Patsy or Annie or Nancy or whatever your name is, why did you make us come over here?" Brad demanded. "I've only been here for two minutes, and I'm already bored. Can I go now?"

"Me too," Brenda said. She tapped her pen against her notebook. "I am so, so busy working on this case."

"That's it! That's exactly why I asked you all to come," Nancy said with a smile. "Tomorrow is supposed to be the grand opening of the carousel in the park. And so far, no one has found the brass ring!"

"But I am *so* close," Brenda said impatiently. "So can I please go now?"

Nancy ignored Brenda's question. "I have great news. The pressure's off!"

"Huh?" Mia said.

"I mean, we all still have to keep trying to find the missing brass ring," Nancy explained. "But we don't have to find the brass ring by tomorrow. We have another Thomas Gangi brass ring!"

Mia, Jo, and Brenda all gasped at the same time.

"What?" Mia cried out. "What are you talking about, Nancy?"

"Your great-great-great grandfather made three brass rings, including the one that's missing. My dad managed to find another one at an antique store," Nancy said. "I have it in my backpack right now. My dad asked me to give it to your dad when he gets home from work. Then your dad's going to have the brass ring and all the horses moved to the park first thing tomorrow—in time for the opening tomorrow afternoon!"

"Isn't that great news?" Bess chirped.

Everyone started talking all at once. Nancy studied the faces of her three suspects, Brenda and Sam and Brad. Brenda was busy talking and writing in her notebook at the same time. Brad seemed bored. Sam was the only one who looked worried.

Only Nancy, George, and Bess knew that there *was* no second brass ring—not in River Heights, anyway. Nancy's backpack had nothing but books and notebooks in it. Nancy was hoping that the thief, whoever it was, would try to sneak over to the hall closet and look inside her backpack.

Now that her plan was in place, Nancy and her friends would just have to wait. Who would go for Nancy's backpack? Would it be Sam . . . or Brad . . . or Brenda?

Nancy jumped up from the couch. "May I use your phone? I need to call my dad," she fibbed to Mia and Jo.

"You can use the one in the kitchen," Jo replied.

"I'll go with you, Nancy. I need to get a glass of water," George said.

"Me too," Bess said.

The three girls disappeared into the kitchen. Then, quietly, Nancy doubled back to the hallway. Bess and George followed her. The three girls stood behind a large antique cabinet. That way, they could see the hall closet without being seen.

Nancy put her finger to her lips. "Shhhh."

"Shhhh," Bess and George whispered back.

They waited a minute . . . then two minutes . . . then three minutes. Just then they heard footsteps hurrying down the hall.

A figure approached the hall closet and opened the door. The person pulled Nancy's backpack out and began to unzip it.

Nancy stepped out from behind the cabinet. She couldn't believe her eyes.

"Mia?!" Nancy exclaimed. "*You're* the thief?"

Mia screamed and dropped the backpack.

"No way," said Bess, shaking her head.

"But you and your sister are the ones who found the brass ring and the horses to begin with," George pointed out.

Mia stared at the floor. "That's just it," she said after a minute. "I didn't want the horses to go to the park. I wanted to keep them here."

"Did Jo want to keep them here too?" Nancy asked her.

Mia rolled her eyes. "No. Jo thought we should share the horses with everybody. So did Mom and Dad. But how unfair is that? I mean, Jo and I found them!"

"So you decided to steal the brass ring and make everyone think there was a ghost around," Nancy said slowly. "That way, your mom and dad wouldn't be able to give the horses to the city."

Mia nodded. "But I freaked out when you said you had another Thomas Gangi brass ring, Nancy. That would have ruined everything! So I had to hide that one, too."

Sam, Jo, Brad, and Brenda appeared just

then. "Who screamed? What's going on?" Brenda demanded. Her pen was poised over her notebook.

Nancy filled the four of them in.

Jo gasped. "Mia! You're the thief?" she cried out when Nancy had finished.

Mia's lip trembled. "I couldn't say good-bye to our horses. I just couldn't!" she moaned.

Jo ran up and hugged her sister. "Oh, poor Mia! Mom and Dad are going to be soooooo mad. But don't worry, I'll stand up for you."

"What about the muddy footprints and the music?" Nancy asked Mia.

Mia frowned. "I planted the footprints and the initials before you guys came over," she explained. "Then I went down to the basement while I was supposed to be getting ready for my violin lesson. I hid a portable CD player behind some furniture and used a remote control." She added, "I was trying to spook you guys, plus make someone else look guilty. Like Brad."

"Oh, thanks a lot. Just for that, I'm taking your Christmas present back to the store," Brad grumbled. Then he broke into a grin.

"Still, I have to say, you aren't as lame as I thought, Mia! That's pretty cool, pulling off a crime wave!"

Mia blushed. "I did *not* pull off a crime wave," she muttered.

"So I guess it was just a coincidence that your mom and dad had a CD with that song too," George said to Brad.

Sam was plucking at his T-shirt. "What about you, Sam?" Nancy said. "Did you help your sister with all this?"

Sam stared at her, his green eyes enormous. "No!" he cried out. "I knew about it, though. I saw Mia do it! I didn't want to—" He stopped.

"Tell on her?" Brenda asked him from the corner. She had been furiously writing in her notebook.

"Samster the Hamster," Brad said. "My man!" He grabbed Sam around the shoulders and squeezed him playfully.

George turned to Mia. "So where's the real brass ring?" she asked her.

"I think I know," Nancy said with a twinkle in her eye.

Everyone stared at her. "You do?" Jo asked.

Nancy nodded. "Yup! I found a really important clue on a Web site about Thomas Gangi. It gave me an idea about Mia's hiding place for the brass ring."

Nancy began running to the library. She tried to slow her steps, but she was too excited. The others followed close behind.

When Nancy got to the library, she rushed up to the horses. She began running her hands over each and every one.

When she got to the twelfth horse, she found what she was looking for. There was a hairline crack on the horse's side. She ran her fingers across the crack. It was a secret compartment!

"Bess was right," Mia said after a minute. "Nancy's an awesome detective! She found where I hid the brass ring."

Nancy took her barrette out of her hair and wiggled it carefully into the crack. There was a popping sound and the compartment creaked open.

Nancy reached inside and felt cold, smooth metal. She pulled it out.

She'd found the brass ring!

***

Wednesday afternoon was sunny and warm. A crisp breeze tossed Nancy's blond hair as she and the other children climbed up onto the carousel horses.

Nancy picked the one with the four calling birds. George picked the one with the seven swams a-swimming. Bess chose the one with the three French hens.

Mr. Drew, Hannah, and Mr. and Mrs. Gangi stood outside the glass walls, waving like mad. George's parents and Bess's parents were there too.

The mayor of River Heights was standing in the doorway of the carousel. "Welcome to our brand-new carousel!" he exclaimed. "Thanks to the Gangi family, the city of River Heights will be able to enjoy this carousel for many years to come."

The crowd clapped. Jo and Mia smiled at each other. Nancy knew that Mia had told their parents what she had done and had apologized lots and lots of times. Mr. and Mrs. Gangi had forgiven Mia and had let her come to the carousel opening.

Mia had also apologized to Nancy, George, and Bess. What Mia had done was wrong.

But Nancy knew that Mia felt really bad about it.

Music started to play. It was "The Twelve Days of Christmas"! Lights flashed, bells jingled, and the horses began to move. Nancy couldn't believe it. It was really happening. Thomas Gangi's old carousel had come to life after all these years.

The brass ring hung from the side of the carousel with its delicate mistletoe design. All the children reached for it when their horses passed by. But the brass ring was hard to get.

Nancy reached for it her first time around . . . then her second . . . and her third. Each time, her fingers brushed against the ring. But she didn't have enough time to grab it. The carousel was going way too fast.

The fourth time around, Nancy sat up in her saddle just a little—as far as her safety strap would let her. She reached her arm as far as she could. Her fingertips brushed the ring and then she grabbed it!

"Nancy Drew got the ring!" the mayor announced.

The crowd cheered and cheered. Nancy giggled excitedly. She had grabbed the brass ring! And it was the very same brass ring she had found just yesterday, hidden in a secret compartment.

The song began to fade. The horses slowed to a stop. The attendant came around and unstrapped all the children. Nancy jumped off her horse and ran to her father.

Mr. Drew grabbed her in a big hug. "Congratulations, Pudding Pie! You grabbed the brass ring!"

"She's a girl of many talents!" Hannah said proudly.

The mayor handed Nancy a box. "This is your special prize for grabbing the brass ring. Congratulations!"

Bess and George gathered around Nancy. "What is it?" Bess asked Nancy eagerly.

Nancy reached into the box. Inside was a music box—shaped like a carousel!

"Oh, thank you, Mr. Mayor!" Nancy exclaimed. "It's the best music box ever!"

"It's the perfect prize for the detective who solved the mystery of the missing brass ring!" George said.

That night, Nancy sat at her desk and wrote in her blue notebook:

Today I got to ride on the new carousel. I grabbed the brass ring and won a special prize. It's a carousel music box. It's the best prize I've ever gotten!

I'm glad we found the brass ring. This was a really tough mystery to solve. It was tough because thieves usually steal things that don't belong to them. But in this case, the thief, Mia, stole something that *did* belong to her and her family. She just wanted to keep the horses for herself and her family.

But now Mia will get to ride the carousel whenever she wants in the park. And other kids will get to ride the carousel too—thanks to the Gangi family. Jo and her mom and dad were right after all. It's best to share, because if you share, everyone's happy—including you!

Case closed!